Six stories about how people's lives, and relationships, change when they encounter a

Fork in the Road

"Said the Unicorn" -- Tessa dedicates herself to her Master's service, so his determination to add another woman to their family devastates her.

"Proposals" -- The evening appears perfectly arranged for him to pop the question. But, Christopher's proposition takes Geraldine on an unanticipated sexual adventure.

"Winners & Losers" -- When he finally walks away from the blackjack table, Jeffrey finds someone worth gambling on.

I.G. Frederick trades words for cash, specializing in erotic fiction and poetry since 2001. Her erotic short stories appear in Hustler Fantasies, Forum, Foreplay, and Desire Presents, as well as electronic, audio, and print anthologies. Her novels receive high praise from readers, critics, and other authors.

A FemDom, Ms. Frederick, owns the man she adores. Although dominant in the rest of his life, he demonstrates his love by serving as her submissive. Ms. Frederick often writes about finding love in BDSM relationships from the authority of one enjoying that for almost a decade.

http://eroticawriter.net/

How lives change
when they encounter a

fork in
the Road

I.G. Frederick

Author of Dommemoir & Second Chances

Fork in the Road
© **2014 by I.G. Frederick**

ISBN: 978-1937471-19-4

Pussy Cat Press
http://pussycatpress.com/publisher.html/
P.O. Box 19764
Portland OR 97280

First published electronically in 2013

Table of Contents

Proposals
What a Tangled Web We Weave

By I.G. Frederick

Through the glass, Geraldine watched the tall dark-skinned man stride across the parking garage toward the restaurant elevator. Dressed up for the occasion, he wore a black jacket, black shirt, and white tie. At better than six-feet tall, Christopher's height almost overwhelmed her when they were together, even though she was almost five seven herself. But he was the sweetest, gentlest man she had ever met and she had come to love him dearly over the last six months.

Three of her friends were betting that Christopher would propose tonight. He'd made reservations at one of the most elegant restaurants in town and told her they needed to have a serious discussion. But Geraldine suspected something else. Despite his charm, she sensed Chris was keeping something secret from her. She hoped tonight he would tell her what so she could decide whether or not it was a deal breaker.

"Wow, you look fantastic, Gerry." Chris leaned down to kiss her on the cheek.

She turned her face so their lips met, bracing herself with a hand on his muscular arm for the thrill his touch sent through her body. Mint mouthwash on his breath tickled her nose, adding to the sensory deluge. The past three days she'd tried to imagine what he could be hiding from her, hoping it wouldn't destroy their relationship. She had never enjoyed a man's company as much as Christopher's, but if his secret was so devastating he believed he couldn't confide in her ... well, she would suffer less if she broke it off now.

Roger was convinced Chris was still married Loretta certain he'd decided he was gay, despite Gerry's reports of amazing sexual chemistry. And, of course everyone else believed he had planned some sort of elaborate, romantic proposal.

Chris offered her his arm and they rode up thirty floors. The elevator doors slid open and a wave of tantalizing aromas washed over them -- garlic and ginger, sizzling steak, and fried seafood. The waiter led them to a table covered in crisp white linen next to the wall of windows. With the city straddling the river far below them, Gerry silently wished the majority of her friends were correct, even though until she met Chris she had no interest in getting married again.

Chris let the view hold his attention, sharing his observations about various landmarks, until their drinks arrived. He toyed with his martini glass, twirling the yellow concoction around and around while she sipped at the combination of fruit juices and rum in her mai tai.

"Geraldine, I don't know if you realize how fond I've become of you."

Interesting choice of words, fond. And using her full name didn't bode well.

"I really would like to take our relationship to the next level." He gulped down half his margarita in one swallow.

"But?" She plucked the cherry from her glass and bit it off the stem.

He rested his folded hands on the table. "But, I've been married twice before, and I've finally learned that without certain," he cleared his throat, "elements, I can't..." he took another gulp, "I just can't."

Does that mean you want to marry me, if...? "Perhaps you should tell me what these "elements" are?" She drew air quotes.

"Can I interest you two in some appetizers? Some Black Tiger Shrimp Tempura or a Spicy Yellowfin Tuna Roll?"

What timing. "Could you give us a few minutes?"She tapped the thick leather volume in front of her. "We haven't even had a chance to look at the menu."

The waiter disappeared and Gerry scrutinized Chris, tilting her head to one side.

He leaned forward and whispered, "I'm a pervert."

"That's rather a broad classification. Can you be more specific?"

His chin dropped to his chest. She could see his mouth move, but couldn't hear his words over the tinkle of piano music from the bar and the chatter of other diners.

"Would you like to text it to me?"

She *was* joking, but gratitude infused his features and he grinned, pulling out his cell. Gerry had turned off her ringer, but she extracted her phone from her purse and stared wide-eyed at the message he sent.

"I take it from your expression, this is not something you've been involved in before?" His deep voice broke through her shock.

She shook her head and took a long swallow of rum-infused fruit juice. Opening her menu, she blinked until she could focus on the words. "Maybe we should order some food?" She didn't think alcohol caused her dizziness, but putting something substantial in her stomach wouldn't hurt.

They stared out the window without speaking until the waiter set a plate of Kung Pao Calamari on the table between them and the scent of onions and ginger steamed around her. Gerry speared a ring and dipped it into the Hoisin sauce before popping it into her mouth. The spicy combination woke up her senses and her curiosity. "How much do you need this? Just in the bedroom or all the time?"

Chris blinked rapidly, staring at her. "I could settle for the former, but would much prefer the latter."

She took another succulent piece of the breaded calamari and skipped the spicy sauce. Chris sat with his hands in his lap, avoiding her eyes.

"You should try these, they're delicious."

"Thank you." He pulled a few pieces onto his plate and spooned some of the sauce over them. He swallowed and looked at her with pleading eyes. "Would you consider ...?" He pressed his thick lips together.

She took a deep breath. "I don't know much about it."

He grinned, revealing white, even teeth. "I could teach you. There are all kinds of books, I have more than a few myself. And there's groups in town where you could meet others who ..."

She cleared her throat. "*If* I decide to explore this, I prefer we keep it between us." She couldn't even imagine telling her friends, never mind joining a group with a bunch of strangers.

"If that's what you wish, Ma'am."

Gerry blinked rapidly, trying to find her equilibrium and seriously considered a trip to the ladies' room that ended at the elevator. "Let's stick to names, for now. At least in public."

Disappointment flashed across his face, but he swallowed and it disappeared.

When their entrées arrived, Chris sat with his hands on his lap while Gerry cut into her macadamia encrusted pork chop and savored flavors of rich nuts and tender meat drizzled with vanilla infused passion fruit sauce. She helped herself to a taste of Chris's goat cheese and prosciutto stuffed chicken and sampled his buttermilk mashed potatoes with lemon garlic jus that melted on her tongue. "Not bad. You'll like it."

Only then, did he pick up his knife and fork. She took a deep breath at the implications. *You can do this.*

When the waiter brought the dessert menus, Chris left his sitting on the table. Gerry tilted her head, but he stared at his hands. She couldn't decide between the coconut marjolaine and the crème brûlée so she ordered one for herself and one for Chris. After tasting both, twice, she traded the plates so he had the crème brûlée. He raised his eyes, she nodded, and he dipped his spoon into the creamy concoction.

Gerry was surprised to realize her breathing had become shallow and her heart was racing. More than anything else, she wanted to take Chris home and rip off his clothes. After he paid the bill, she rose to her feet and strode toward the elevator. She heard his heavy footsteps following her and they rode down to the garage in silence.

He handed her into his red Acura and slid behind the wheel. "Where to, Ma'am?"

She took a deep breath. "If we go back to your place, will I be surprised by things you haven't shown me before besides these books you apparently have stashed away somewhere?"

He looked down. "Yes, Ma'am."

"Don't think I'm ready for that. Take me home."

His lips tightened in a grimace, but he started the car, backed out, and headed toward the exit.

Watching the line of red lights stretch out in front of them across the Burnside Bridge and the white lights coming in the other direction, Gerry wondered if she was cut out for the kind of relationship Chris said he wanted. For that matter, he seemed too willful, independent, and stubborn. One thing to have a man willingly "devote myself to your pleasure," as he'd texted. Another to force him to obey.

When he pulled up in front of her building's entrance, Chris spoke for the first time since he'd started the car. "Would, Ma'am like me to come in after I park?"

"You'd better." Whatever the evening's outcome, Gerry intended to at least get laid.

By the time she unlocked her condo, turned on the lights, and closed all the window blinds, Chris stood in the doorway. She tilted her head to look up at him. "Aren't you supposed to be on your knees or something?"

He closed the door. "Yes, Ma'am. Would you like me naked, as well."

Gerry smiled. "Why not?"

Chris loosened his tie, removed his jacket, and slipped out of the black silk shirt that clung to his lean torso. Hanging them all on one arm of her bentwood coat tree, he stripped down to black bikini briefs and socks, then lowered himself to his knees.

Gerry pointed at his crotch. "I think you forgot something."

Chris's wide nose flared. She found his fear incredibly endearing. He added his briefs to the pile on the tree and stuffed his socks in his shoes. His cock pointed straight out at her and Gerry licked her lips.

After he knee-walked over to her, Chris leaned over, and kissed her feet. The touch of his lips on the skin exposed by the slinky sandals she still wore, sent a charge coursing through Gerry. Suppressing a shudder, she grabbed his ear and pulled him up so she could look into his dark brown eyes.

She leaned down to kiss him and he tilted his head back. On a whim, she bit his lower lip, sinking her teeth into the thick moist flesh. She wasn't sure which surprised her more, his reaction or hers. He moaned and swayed, his eyes rolling back into his head. Her panties got wet and she shivered with need. Realizing if she wanted to have sex with Chris all she had to do was demand it, Gerry tightened her grip on his ear and dragged him toward the bedroom. Despite staying on his knees, Chris kept up with her. She wondered if he would get rug burns, then decided she didn't care. *He's the one who wants this.*

Gerry sat on the edge of the bed and raised her feet off the floor. Chris slipped off first one sandal and then the other, slowly kissing each foot from toes to ankle as he did so, caressing her skin with his lips. Now her eyes were the ones rolling back. Her breathing came in audible gasps. Chris looked up with a glint in his eye, one corner of his mouth raised higher than the other.

He dragged a finger from her ankle to the top of her thigh. "Would Ma'am like me to continue?"

She hooked one foot behind his head and pulled him closer. Starting at her knees, he licked every inch of her bare skin until, burying his head under the narrow skirt of her black dress, he finally reached her soaked panties and inhaled deeply. Even she could smell her arousal. She lifted her hips and he dragged the black cotton slowly down her legs. She draped her thighs over his shoulders, pressing her heels against his naked back, urging him forward.

One of the things she had always loved about sex with Chris was his appetite for oral, but he outdid himself tonight. He engulfed her clit in his thick lips until she cried out, then he pushed his tongue deep into her. In the past she felt guilty about how long his face stayed between her legs sending her into paroxysm of pleasure. She always believed she had to give as much as she took. But, now she just reveled in the attention, letting him lick her lips inside and out, nuzzle her clit with his tongue, and thrust its entire length into the heat of her core.

When her clit throbbed at the edge of over sensitivity, she pushed him away with her feet against on his shoulders. He sat back on his heels and licked her juices off his lips. "Thank you, Ma'am, that was delicious." His cock still pointed straight up.

Gerry just stared at him, wondering what he would do if she crawled under the covers and went to sleep.

"Would Ma'am like me to give her a massage? Or a bath? Perhaps, she wishes to go to sleep while keeping me available to serve her in the morning? I make a mean omelette."

As tempting as his suggestions sounded, there was only one thing Gerry wanted at the moment. She opened the drawer of the nightstand, dug out a condom, and tossed it at him.

"Yes, Ma'am. Thank you, Ma'am."

She sat up and eased her slinky black dress over her head, tossing it onto the arm chair in the corner. Still wearing her bra slip, she got up on her knees and patted the bed. Chris stretched out on his back and she threw one leg over his hips. He ran his hands up her thighs and caressed her ass through the silky fabric of her slip. With one hand, Gerry rubbed the head of his cock against her clit and trembled at her reaction. Already hypersensitive, the soft skin of his glans against her swollen flesh almost sent her over the edge again.

Unable to resist any longer, she guided him into position and sank down onto his cock, sighing with pleasure. For a moment, she stayed still, reveling in the sensations of a full pussy, his coarse pubic hair tickling her lips. She admired the lean muscular body between her legs with the new understanding that it was available to serve her every whim. A wide grin split his face and he looked up at her adoringly.

Already floating in post-orgasmic euphoria from the magic he worked with his tongue, she didn't have the strength to move. "Make me come."

"Yes, Ma'am. Thank you, Ma'am."

Holding onto her hips, Chris raised and lowered himself, pushing up into her. She smiled. This pervert stuff had some definite benefits. He maneuvered his big hand so he could tease her clit with his thumb while moving his hips up and down so he massaged her internally with his cock. Gerry groaned, finding it more and more difficult to stay upright. When he sent her trembling off into another orgasm, she collapsed on his chest. He stroked her ass and back until she stopped shaking.

Unable to open her eyes, Gerry slid off him onto the bed. Using Chris's shoulder as a pillow while his hand caressed her backside, she found herself drifting toward sleep. With difficulty, she managed to open one eye wide enough to see his sheathed erection still pointing straight up. A smile tickled her lips.

Tomorrow she would have to get a list of the "all kinds of books" Chris had mentioned so she could learn more about this pervert stuff. But, she was pretty sure she liked the concept and if she allowed Chris to marry her, she'd be the wife he stuck with.

Proposals
When First We
Practice to Deceive

By I.G. Frederick

Through the glass, Geraldine watched the tall dark-skinned man stride across the parking garage toward the restaurant elevator. Dressed up for the occasion, he wore a black jacket, black shirt, and white tie. At better than six-feet tall, Christopher's height almost overwhelmed her when they were together, even though she was almost five, seven herself. But he was the sweetest, gentlest man she had ever met and she had come to love him dearly over the last six months.

Three of her friends were betting that Christopher would propose tonight. He'd made reservations at one of the most elegant restaurants in town and told her they needed to have a serious discussion. But Geraldine suspected something else. Despite his charm, she sensed Chris was keeping something secret from her. She hoped tonight he would tell her what so she could decide whether or not it was a deal breaker.

"You look fantastic, Gerry." Chris leaned down to kiss her on the cheek.

She turned her face so their lips met, bracing herself with a hand on his muscular arm for the thrill his touch sent through her body. Mint mouthwash on his breath tickled her nose, adding to the sensory deluge. The past three days she'd tried to imagine what he could be hiding from her, hoping it wouldn't destroy their relationship. She had never enjoyed a man's company as much as Christopher's, but if his secret was so devastating he believed he couldn't confide in her ... well, she would suffer less if he broke it off now.

Roger was convinced Chris was still married. Loretta certain he'd decided he was gay, despite Gerry's reports of amazing sexual chemistry. And, of course everyone else believed he had planned some sort of elaborate, romantic proposal.

Chris offered her his arm and they rode up thirty floors. The elevator doors slid open and a wave of tantalizing aromas washed over them -- garlic and ginger, sizzling steak, and fried seafood. The waiter led them to a table covered in crisp white linen next to the wall of windows. With the city straddling the river far below them, Gerry silently wished the majority of her friends were correct, even though until she met Chris she had no interest in getting married again.

Chris let the view hold his attention, sharing his observations about various landmarks, until their drinks arrived. He toyed with his martini glass, twirling the yellow concoction around and around while she sipped at the combination of fruit juices and rum in her mai tai.

"Geraldine, I don't know if you realize how fond I've become of you."

Interesting choice of words, fond. And using her full name didn't bode well.

"I really would like to take our relationship to the next level." He gulped down half his margarita in one swallow.

"But?" She plucked the cherry from her glass and bit it off the stem.

He rested his folded hands on the table. "But, I've been married twice before, and I've finally learned that without certain," he cleared his throat, "elements, I can't..." he took another gulp, "I just can't."

Does that mean you want to marry me, if ...? "Perhaps you could tell me what these "elements" are?" She drew air quotes.

"Can I interest you two in some appetizers? Some Black Tiger Shrimp Tempura or a Spicy Yellowfin Tuna Roll?"

What timing.

"Could you could give us a few minutes?"He tapped the thick leather volume in front of him. "We haven't even had a chance to peruse the menu."

The waiter disappeared and Gerry scrutinized Chris, tilting her head to one side.

He leaned forward, winked, and whispered, "I'm a pervert."

"That's kind of a broad classification. Can you be a bit more specific?"

He grinned, revealing white, even teeth, and a wicked glint lit up his eyes.

Her eyes opened wide and her jaw dropped.

Leaning across the table, he put one finger under her chin and pulled her face towards his so he could whisper in her ear. "I'm a Dominant. I want to put you on your knees and take control of you. I would love to tie you up and whip your ass before I fuck your brains out."

Geraldine sat back in her chair. She could feel the color draining from her face.

"I take it from your expression, this is not something you've been involved in before?"

She shook her head and took a long swallow of rum-infused fruit juice. Opening her menu, she blinked until she could focus on the words. "Maybe we could order some food?" She didn't think alcohol caused her dizziness, but putting something substantial in her stomach wouldn't hurt.

They stared out the window without speaking until the waiter set a plate of Kung Pao Calamari on the table between them and the scent of onions and ginger steamed around her. Chris speared a ring and dipped it into the Hoisin sauce before holding the fork in front of her mouth. The spicy combination woke up her senses and her curiosity. "How much do you need this? Just in the bedroom or all the time?"

One corner of Chris's mouth lifted and he undressed her with his eyes. "I could settle for the former, but would much prefer the latter."

She helped herself to another succulent piece of the breaded calamari, skipping the spicy sauce.

Chris pulled a few pieces onto his plate and spooned some of the sauce over them. He smiled at her. "Would you consider ...?"

She took a deep breath. "I don't know much about it."

He grinned. "I could teach you. If you're interested, there are all kinds of books, I have more than a few myself. And there's groups in town where you could meet others you can learn from."

She cleared her throat. "*If* I decide to explore this, I prefer we keep it between us." She couldn't even imagine telling her friends, never mind joining a group with a bunch of strangers.

"For now."

Gerry blinked rapidly, trying to find her equilibrium, wondering if she should flee. She could pretend she needed to use the ladies' room...

When their entrées arrived, Chris sampled both, then switched the plates giving Gerry the macadamia encrusted pork chop, taking the goat cheese and prosciutto stuffed chicken for himself.

She took a deep breath, but discovered she very much enjoyed the flavors of rich nuts and tender meat combined with vanilla infused passion fruit sauce..

When the waiter brought the dessert menus, Chris grabbed them both. Gerry glared at him, but he ordered crème brûlée for himself and coconut marjolaine for her.

Gerry was surprised to realize her breathing had become shallow and her heart was racing. More than anything else, she wanted Chris to take her home and rip off her clothes. After he paid the bill, he pulled her to her feet and guided her toward the elevator with a hand at the small of her back. They rode down to the garage in silence.

He handed her into his red Acura, slid behind the wheel and turned the car toward the exit.

Watching the line of red lights stretch out in front of them across the Burnside Bridge and the white lights coming in the other direction, Gerry wondered if she was cut out for the kind of relationship Chris said he wanted. For that matter, he seemed too gentle and considerate. One thing to have a man force her to submit to his will, another for him to expect her to serve him willingly.

He parked the car in the garage under his building. She stayed frozen in her seat until he opened her door and reached one hand inside. Placing her small hand in his bigger one, she let him pull her from the car. Whatever the evening's outcome, at least Gerry could hope to get laid.

At the door of his condo, Chris turned to her. "Once we go inside, I'm your Master. I know you're new at this and I will take that into consideration. If it ever becomes too intense, if you ever need me to back off or even to stop, just say spider-web."

She stared at him, wondering what he had done with her sweet Christopher.

When the door closed behind them, he pulled out the sticks holding her long blond hair in a bun, ran his fingers through its length, and grabbed a fistful of it at the base of her neck. Tugging gently, he guided her down to her knees.

Sinking into the plush carpet, she was embarrassed to realize her panties were soaked.

He leaned down and kissed her. "You can't imagine how long I've wanted to see you there or how much it turns me on."

The latter wasn't difficult to envision as his cock was tenting his slacks in her direction. She reached out and eased the zipper down. He released her hair. She extracted him from his black boxers and kissed his glans.

"Good, girl." His voice was husky with need and Gerry was surprised at how turned on she was by her position, the soft silky skin of his cock against her lips, the scratchiness of the carpet pressing into her knees.

She bathed the length of his cock with her tongue, tasting his musk, reveling in the firm flesh filling her mouth. Encircling him with her lips, she slid them down to his kinky public hair and sniggered silently at her own pun. Chris unbuckled his belt and dropped his trousers to the floor. Without releasing his cock, Gerry tugged the elastic of his boxers down below his ass so she could stroke the firm flesh. With her lips tight around his shaft, she pulled back, letting go with a slurp. When he stopped bouncing, she lowered his shorts and plunged him back into her mouth, holding his cheeks so she could push her face tight against his crotch.

Chris stroked her hair, playing with long strands, dropping one and lifting another with his fingers. His silence challenged her. She pressed her tongue up against the bottom of his shaft while squeezing her lips tightly around him. Finally, he pressed one hand against the back of her head and shot his load down her throat. She swallowed eagerly and licked him clean.

Pulling her to her feet with her hair, Chris threw her over his shoulder, stepped out of the clothing gathered around his ankles, and carried her down the hall to his bedroom. He tossed her on the bed which had been stripped of everything but the bottom sheet. Leather cuffs rested a foot in from each corner, attached by chains to something under the bed.

Gerry gasped, but before she could catch her breath, Chris had unzipped her dress and stripped it off her. "I never want to see pantyhose on you again." He pulled it and her oh-so-wet underwear down her legs. "Stockings and garters and if you must wear panties, I prefer thongs."

"I guess." Gerry wondered what she would do with all the pantyhose in her drawer.

"The appropriate response is, Yes, Sir."

Gerry hesitated.

"If you can't manage that, we may as well stop now. Is that what you want?"

"No, Sir." she whispered.

"That's better." He dumped his jacket, tie, and shirt on the dresser and sat on the edge of his bed, pulling her across his legs, her head hanging down on one side, her legs on the other. "This is why I don't like pantyhose. I never want to have to work to get access to your luscious ass. Understand?"

"Yes, Sir."

"Good girl." He caressed her ass with one hand, reaching down to squeeze a tit with the other.

Gerry wriggled with need.

He slapped her across her cheeks, hard. She shrieked, but the pain traveled from her tender ass to her clit.

"You'll move if and when I tell you."

She tried to stay still, but her body betrayed her and her hips wiggled again.

Chris spanked her a dozen times in rapid succession, leaving her gasping for breath. A single tear crept down her cheek. He slid one finger between her thighs, reaching into her moistness. She moaned.

"Such a slut." He wiggled his finger until it almost touched her clit, but stopped short.

She screamed in frustration.

He chuckled and spanked her again.

When do we get to the fuck your brains out part? Gerry didn't dare ask the question out loud, but she so very much needed him to pound into her.

Chris stroked her sore ass and she felt him getting hard against her belly. He pinched her nipple, slowly at first, but harder and harder until she cried out.

Dragging her off his lap on to the bed, he turned her on her back and fastened cuffs around her wrists and ankles. Gerry pulled against the chains but had less than an inch of slack. The leather felt cool against her heated skin and she enjoyed the helplessness of her position. She just hoped Chris planned to get to the fucking part, soon.

He reached into the drawer of his nightstand where he kept his condoms, but extracted a chain with miniature clamps at each end. Attaching first one and then the other to her nipples, he tightened the screws until she felt as if she couldn't breath. He leaned over and whispered in her ear. "Remember, your safeword is spiderweb."

She managed to nod, but didn't think she could speak. Besides, she didn't want him to stop, she wanted him to fuck her. She lifted her hips off the bed and Chris slapped her hard against her mons. She whimpered. He pulled up on the chain, stretching her nipples until she shrieked. Again, she lifted her hips, begging for his cock in her dripping pussy, and again he slapped her down.

"Please, Sir."

"Please what."

"Please, fuck my brains out, Sir."

Much to her relief, Gerry heard a condom package ripping open and Chris knelt between her legs, plunging his sheathed cock deep inside her. She moaned. Chris slammed into her with a fervor he had never demonstrated before and her eyes rolled back in her head, her body reverberating with sensation. Her nipples had gone numb, and the cold metal chain slithered back and forth on her chest as her breasts bounced up and down with the ferocity of Chris's thrusts.

His pubes smashed into her clit until she shook so violently one of the clamps popped free. The pain in her nipple as the blood rushed back into her bruised flesh intensified her orgasm until it consumed her and she was only vaguely aware of Chris groaning and becoming still. He pulled off the other clamp and she screeched and trembled as the most amazing orgasm she had ever experienced finally faded.

He removed the cuffs and gathered her into his arms, cradling her head against his shoulder. A smile tickled her lips. Tomorrow she would have to get a list of the "all kinds of books" Chris had mentioned so she could learn more about this pervert stuff. But, she was pretty sure she liked the concept and that if Chris married her, she'd be the wife he stuck with.

Said the Unicorn Now That We See Each Other

By I.G. Frederick

Tessa waited on her knees for Master to finish his phone call. Although she obediently looked down at the floor, she couldn't help admiring him through her lashes. Master's powerful legs, muscular chest, and well-formed biceps left her weak-kneed and in awe of his dominance.

A strand of her long blond hair drifted over her shoulder. Tessa tossed it back. Master didn't like anything covering her breasts, even her hair which he loved to play with and pull. She straightened her back and thrust her tits forward so her hair would stay behind her shoulders.

Finally Master set the phone on the table next to his big leather armchair. "Now, my pet, where were we?"

"You said you had a request to make of me when the phone rang, Sir."

He chuckled. "It was a rhetorical question, pet. I do remember." He put one finger under her chin and tilted her head back, giving her permission to look in his eyes.

Deep blue, surrounded by dark lashes, they drew her in, making it difficult to concentrate on his words.

"Do you know what a unicorn is, pet?"

That has to be a trick question. "A mythical beast that looks like a white horse with a single horn in the middle of its forehead?"

He laughed and she dropped her chin to her chest. *Wrong answer.*

"That's one definition. But, in this case, I'm referring to an even rarer creature, one that's more difficult to catch. A unicorn is a bisexual woman willing to join an existing couple and become part of their family."

Tessa bit her lip trying to prevent the tears that sprang to her eyes from spilling over. She gasped for breath and tried to push words out of her mouth. "Permission to speak, Sir?"

"Of course."

"Master is displeased with me? I don't serve him adequately? Please, Master, tell me what I've done wrong, how I can do better, why he wants someone else?" A single tear trickled down her cheek and she felt it hanging at the end of her chin before it splashed onto her breast.

Master opened his legs and pulled her between them, cradling her head against his tight abdomen. "You've done nothing wrong, pet, I'm not at all displeased with you. Rather, I think you're progressed far enough in your training that it's time to start looking for a third."

She sobbed.

He stroked her hair. "Pet, you've always known I'm poly, I told you that from the very beginning."

I thought I could learn to serve you so well you wouldn't want another slave

"I just wanted to concentrate on training you, make sure

you were comfortable with my protocols, before I introduced another girl to the mix."

Her tears had soaked his shirt and she tried to pull away so she could go get him a dry one. But, he held her against him, one arm wrapped around her shoulders, the fingers of the other running through the long blond strands that hung halfway down her back.

"Don't worry, pet. You'll always be first in my heart. If you'd like, I'll let you find the slave you want to be your sister, as long as I approve of her, of course."

"I don't want a sister," she wailed, protocols forgotten. "I'm straight."

"I will give you some leeway in how you interact with your sister slave." His stern tone sent an arctic chill through her heart. "But, I have no intention of limiting myself to one woman. I explained that when you first offered yourself to me."

"I can't, I just can't." Tessa almost choked on her tears.

"Do you want some time to think about this?" He pushed her shoulders back until she sat on her heels much further away from the comfort of his arms than she wanted to be.

"Please, Sir."

"You may go to your room."

Tessa hung her head, pushed herself to her feet, and backed away.

𝒰

Tessa ordered a mocha and found an empty table in the small coffee shop that had become all too familiar over the past few weeks. She checked the time on her cell. Blind date number fourteen would be late in three minutes. Master insisted on punctuality and tardiness was on Tessa's list of behavior that made someone unsuitable. She admitted that list had gotten rather long, but Master was being patient. If she had to accept another woman in his home, she wanted to make sure it was someone she could at least be friends with.

The bells over the glass door jangled and a stunning brunette entered. Tessa held her breath. She really didn't need someone more beautiful to compete for Master's attention. The woman had thick black hair almost as long as Tessa's. Black eyeliner accented startling blue eyes under flawlessly arched eyebrows that slashed across creamy skin. Pink lipstick shone from perfect cupid bow lips and black nail polish gleamed from surprisingly short, but perfectly shaped, nails. She wore a black halter top that showed off an impressive cleavage and leather pants accenting slender hips. Tessa wondered how Master would feel about the industrials in the woman's right ear. She also wore a collection of leather bracelets on both wrists and large silver tear-drop earrings.

The woman approached Tessa's table just as the barista called out her name, so she couldn't exactly pretend to be someone else. "Hi, I'm Marie. Let me get that for you."

Marie paid for her own drink and brought Tessa's mocha to the table, setting it in front of her with a subtle bow. She pointed to the chair across from Tessa and gave her a querying look. Tessa nodded and she sat down.

"I hope you don't mind me saying, you're so very pretty." Tessa blushed.

"I love your hair. And your eyes. I would definitely call that emerald green."

The barista called her name and Marie went to get her coffee. She stood by her chair until Tessa nodded before she sat down again.

"I can't tell you how excited I am at the prospect of becoming part of a family again. I'm so very tired of being alone."

Tessa sipped at her rich chocolate-coffee combination. "You never did say what happened to your previous family."

"I don't like to talk about it. I was driving. Even though it wasn't my fault ..." Marie dropped her eyes. "Master sat beside me in the passenger seat and my sister slave, Laura, behind him." She drank some of her coffee but even after she set the cup back down she didn't speak. After a minute, she said. "The man who hit us was drunk. He ran a stop sign and t-boned the passenger side." All color had drained from her face. She toyed with the handle of her coffee cup. "Master and Laura were killed instantly. I was in the hospital almost two weeks."

Her lips trembled. "He spent less than a year in jail." She looked up, tears glistening in her eyes. "He took everything from me and he didn't even go to prison."

Tessa reached across the table, put her hand over Marie's, and squeezed gently. Marie looked up and the corners of her mouth lifted slightly then dropped again. "Master and Laura were married and he didn't have a will. Her family took everything, the house, the second car, all the furniture. They left me with nothing, just my clothing." She grabbed her cup and gulped down more of her coffee. "It's been almost two years. It still hurts, but I think I'm finally ready to move on." She turned her hand so she could hold Tessa's.

Tessa sipped her mocha. "Do you have questions for me?"

Marie nodded. "How did you meet your Master?"

Tessa smiled. "I was a gift. My first Master trained me but never collared me. He said he was too old for me. Master was his protégée. He gave me to him for Master's birthday with the condition that if Master didn't keep me, he would return me. I'm so grateful Master has found me worthy of his collar." Tessa touched the leather band buckled around her neck, the tag that proclaimed his ownership nestled in the hollow of her throat.

Marie smiled. "What a lovely story. You're so fortunate. I had several bad relationships before I met Master and Laura." She pressed her lips together. "One man claimed to be a Dom, but Master said he was just an abusive stalker."

Tessa suppressed an urge to pull Marie into her arms and comfort her."Would you like to come home and meet Master?" Marie would be the first girl she introduced to Master. She hoped he liked her as much as she did.

𝒰

When Tessa entered the vestibule off the garage, she pulled off her jeans and tank top, hanging them on the hooks on the wall, and kicked off her sandals. She turned to find Marie had already removed her top and was unzipping her leather pants. She had a black thorny rose tattooed on her breast. Tessa hesitated, but Master had never said how he expected her to introduce any prospects to him and he didn't allow her to wear clothing in his house. Perhaps Marie stripping was for the best.

She led the other woman into Master's study and knelt on the plush carpet at his feet, waiting for him to put down his book. Marie fell to her knees on Tessa's left and bent over so her face rested on the carpet her arms above her head. She had a tat of a jaguar striding across her kidneys on her back.

When Master peered at her over his reading glasses, Tessa said, "Sir, may I present Marie. She's interested in serving you and being my sister slave."

"Good girl." Master reached forward and grabbed a fistful of Marie's hair, pulling her into a kneeling position. He pulled some of Tessa's golden hair across Marie's ebony locks. "Nice. I like the contrast."

He turned to Marie. "Tessa's obviously comfortable enough to bring you home. She shared your experience with me before the two of you met and she can train you to meet my needs. So, the only question is how good are you?"

Marie crawled forward and Tessa cringed. This was the part she knew would hate most -- watching anyone else please her Master. Marie unzipped his fly and extracted his already semi-erect cock from his boxers. "Thank you, Sir." She kissed his glans and licked the length of his rod from pubes to tip until it stood straight up.

Weighing his heavy sack in one hand, she grasped the base of his cock in the other and plunged her lips down his shaft to her fingers. Master gasped and Tessa had to bite her lip to keep from bursting into tears.

Master stroked Marie's long, black hair. He crooked a finger of his other hand at Tessa and she crawled over to him, grateful he was even aware of her presence. While Marie's head bobbed up and down, Master grabbed a hunk of Tessa's hair and pulled her up so he could suck on her tit. He released Marie and grabbed Tessa's other nipple, twisting it until she gasped. So slowly that she didn't notice at first, his teeth sunk into the one in his mouth. Her breathing grew heavy and she could smell her own musk as well as Marie's. Hers had much more of a rich vanilla aroma than Tessa's own that Master always described as honey sweet.

When Master came, Marie swallowed every drop. Tessa tried not to pout, but her lower lip crept out from her upper.

"Good, girl." Master patted Marie on the head. "Now, I want to see you two together."

"But, Sir?" Tessa sank back onto her heels.

"It's okay, pet." He reached out his hand and she rested her cheek against his palm. "You don't have to go muff diving since you're straight. You can close your eyes and pretend it's whoever you want between your legs."

"You, of course, Sir."

He chuckled and looked at Marie who had a big grin on her face.

"Thank you, Sir." She opened her arms and Tessa sighed and crawled into them. Marie's touch was delicate and Tessa was surprised to discover she liked the feel of another pair of tits pressed up against her own. Marie ran her hand up and down Tessa's back and stroked the sensitive flesh of her ass until she gasped. Tilting Tessa's chin up, Marie touched her lips to Tessa's. At first, she kept them tightly together, but Marie teased with her tongue until Tessa relented and parted them.

Marie tasted of coffee and peppermint. She ran her tongue along the inside of Tessa's lips while fondling one breast until she was gasping for breath. Easing her back onto the carpet, Marie kissed her way down Tessa's neck to her breasts, tickling them all over with the tip of her tongue and suckling on her nipples. Tessa suppressed the urge to wriggle her hips. Master didn't allow that.

Finally, Marie made her way along Tessa's belly to her cunt. Marie pulled her lips apart and dragged the full length of her tongue through Tessa's slit. She almost screamed. The woman had a piercing near the back of her tongue. When the ball hit Tessa's clit, she had to dig her fingers into the carpet to keep from coming. "Please, Sir," she gasped.

"You have permission to come as much as you want when you're with this one, pet."

Tessa let go and her body shook under Marie's expert ministrations. She convulsed on the carpet as Marie tormented her clit and thrust her tongue deep into Tessa's cunt. Vaguely aware of Master's scent, Tessa opened her mouth and he pushed his cock between her lips. Unable to give him the attention he deserved, she just kept her mouth shaped like an O so he could face fuck her while Marie kept stimulating the orgasm that wouldn't end. Tessa was still trembling when he shot his load deep into her throat and she had to concentrate on swallowing so she wouldn't choke.

"Nice." Master lifted her up into his arms and held her against his chest.

Marie wrapped her arms around Tessa and Master, pressing her breasts against Tessa's back. Tessa clung to Master, but no longer questioned her place in his heart. He had room enough for both of them, and as long as she came first with him, she would find room in hers.

Said the Unicorn
If You Believe in Me, I Believe in You
By I.G. Frederick

Tessa waited on her knees for Master to finish his phone call. Although she obediently looked down at the floor, she couldn't help admiring him through her lashes. Master's powerful legs, muscular chest, and well-formed biceps left her weak-kneed and in awe of his dominance.

A strand of her long blond hair drifted over her shoulder. Tessa tossed it back. Master didn't like anything covering her breasts, even her hair which he loved to play with and pull. She straightened her back and thrust her tits forward so her hair would stay behind her shoulders.

Finally Master set the phone on the table next to his big leather armchair. "Now, my pet, where were we?"

"You said you had a request to make of me when the phone rang, Sir."

He chuckled. "It was a rhetorical question, pet. I remember." He put one finger under her chin and tilted her head back, giving her permission to look in his eyes.

Deep blue, surrounded by dark lashes, they drew her in, making it difficult to concentrate on his words.

"Do you know what a unicorn is, pet?"

That has to be a trick question. "A mythical beast that looks like a white horse with a single horn in the middle of its forehead?"

He laughed and she dropped her chin to her chest. *Wrong answer.*

"That's one definition. But, in this case, I'm referring to an even rarer creature, one that's more difficult to catch. A unicorn is a bisexual woman willing to join an existing couple and become part of their family."

Tessa bit her lip trying to prevent the tears that sprang to her eyes from spilling over. She gasped for breath and tried to push words out of her mouth. "Permission to speak, Sir?"

"Of course."

"Master is displeased with me? I don't serve him adequately? Please, Master, tell me what I've done wrong, how I can do better, why he wants someone else?" A single tear trickled down her cheek and she felt it hanging at the end of her chin before it splashed onto her breast.

Master opened his legs and pulled her between them, cradling her head against his tight abdomen. "You've done nothing wrong, pet, I'm not at all displeased with you. Rather, I think you're progressed far enough in your training that it's time to start looking for a third."

She sobbed.

He stroked her hair. "Pet, you've always known I'm poly, I told you that from the very beginning."

I thought I could learn to serve you so well you wouldn't want another slave.

"I just wanted to concentrate on training you, make sure you were comfortable with my protocols, before I introduced another girl to the mix."

Her tears had soaked his shirt and she tried to pull away so she could go get him a dry one. But, he held her against him, one arm wrapped around her shoulders, the fingers of the other running through the long blond strands that hung halfway down her back.

"Don't worry, pet. You'll always be first in my heart. If you'd like, I'll let you find the slave you want to be your sister, as long as I approve of her, of course."

"I don't want a sister," she wailed, protocols forgotten. "I'm straight."

"I will give you some leeway in how you interact with your sister slave." His stern tone sent an arctic chill through her heart. "But, I have no intention of limiting myself to one woman. I explained that when you first offered yourself to me."

"I can't, I just can't." Tessa almost choked on her tears.

"Do you want some time to think about this?" He pushed her shoulders back until she sat on her heels much further away from the comfort of his arms than she wanted to be.

She shook her head.

"You realize this means I will release you?"

Tessa flung herself at his legs, clinging to them. "Please, Sir, no." But, his fingers unbuckled the leather collar around her neck and set it on the table next to his phone. The gold tag that said she was his property caught the light from the lamp and taunted her.

"You may go to your room and get dressed." The ice in his voice ripped a hole in her heart. "I would like you to find another place to live as soon as possible, but no later than the beginning of next month."

Tessa hung her head, pushed herself to her feet, and backed away.

ll

The bells over the glass door of the coffee shop jangled

and a stunning brunette entered. Tessa smiled at her. "Afternoon, Ma'am. What can I make for you?" The woman had thick black hair almost as long as Tessa's. Black eyeliner accented startling blue eyes under flawlessly arched eyebrows that slashed across creamy skin. Pink lipstick shone from perfect cupid bow lips and black nail polish gleamed from surprisingly short, but perfectly shaped, nails. She wore a black halter top that showed off an impressive cleavage and leather pants accenting slender hips. The woman had industrials in her right ear, a collection of leather bracelets on both wrists, large silver tear-drop earrings, and a beautiful studded leather collar around her neck.

Tessa touched her throat where the tag proclaiming Master's ownership used to hang. She bit her lip to keep from bursting into tears, but her chin trembled.

"Could I get a mocha, please?"

Tessa nodded, afraid to speak, and turned toward the steamer. The smell of espresso and chocolate wafting from the cup she set on the glass counter offered some comfort. "Three seventy-five, please."

The woman handed Tessa a piece of plastic and she swiped it through the machine. "Did you want a receipt?"

"No thanks." She took a sip of her mocha. "Nice. Strong and rich, just the way I like it. I'm Marie."

"Tessa." She handed the woman back her credit card."

"I hope you don't mind me saying, you're so very pretty."
Tessa blushed.

"I love your hair. And your eyes. I would definitely call that emerald green." She took another sip of coffee and seemed to have no intention of taking a seat in the empty café. Tessa grabbed a cloth and polished the top of the small glass case that held the pastries.

"How long have you worked here?"

Tessa shrugged. "Eight months." *And six days.* Ever since she had to leave Master's house and return in disgrace to his mentor who had given Tessa as a birthday present to the man she had come to adore. She pressed her lips together.

Marie waved her hand. "I take it this isn't where you want to be?"

Tessa shook her head. She hesitated, but the woman wore a collar and a tag. "My Master released me. I live with the man who trained me, but he thinks he's too old for me and ..." She held her hand against her naked throat, trying to regain her composure. "I guess I'm not worthy of his collar, either."

Marie reached over the counter and touched Tessa's shoulder. "I understand. I lost my first Master in a horrible auto accident."

Tessa looked up to see tears glistening in Marie's eyes.

"I was the driver. Even though it wasn't my fault ..."

Tessa swallowed. At least she knew Master was still alive even if she couldn't be with him. She clasped the hand on her shoulder. "How?"

"Master was in the passenger seat and my sister slave, Laura, behind him." Marie drank some of her coffee and set the cup down on the counter top. After a minute, she said. "The man who hit us was drunk. He ran a stop sign and t-boned the passenger side." All color had drained from her face. She released Tessa and toyed with the handle of her coffee cup. "Master and Laura were killed instantly. I was in the hospital almost two weeks."

Her lips trembled. "He spent less than a year in jail." She looked up, tears glistening in her eyes. "He took everything from me and he didn't even go to prison."

Tessa reached across the counter. Marie took her hand and Tessa squeezed gently.

Marie looked up and the corners of her mouth lifted slightly then dropped again. "Master and Laura were married and he didn't have a will. Her family took everything, the house, the second car, all the furniture. They left me with nothing, just my clothing." She grabbed her cup and gulped down more of her coffee. "After almost two years it still hurts. But, I was finally able to move on."

Marie smiled. "When I ventured in search of a new Master, I was very, very careful. I had several bad relationships before I met Master and Laura." She pressed her lips together. "One man claimed to be a Dom, but Master said he was just an abusive stalker."

Tessa suppressed an urge to walk around the counter, pull Marie into her arms, and comfort her. Then she remembered. *At least she has a new Master.* She hung her head. *I'm all alone.*

"My new Master would like to find another girl. I know he'd like you. Do you want to meet him?"

Tessa grabbed the cloth and polished the counter next to the espresso machine, wiping off each apothecary jar displaying tea or candies. "Why are all the best Masters poly?" She looked up at Marie. "I'm not. And, I'm straight."

"I understand the straight part. But why wouldn't you want a sister slave? It's so wonderful having someone to share chores with and talk to when Master's busy or about things he doesn't care about. Master used to let Laura and me go out together by ourselves once a week." Her chin dropped to her chest. "I miss that so very much."

She leaned her elbows on the counter and whispered. "And, you're so hot. I would love to make you come until you scream. If you're straight I wouldn't expect you to reciprocate. Maybe give me a back rub if you felt like it."

Tessa just stared at her until the bells over the glass door tinkled and a man dressed in torn jeans and a Doctor Who tee shirt walked up to the counter. Marie stepped aside until Tessa had made his cappuccino and plated his scone.

"What if you just come home with me and meet Master. We can make him dinner together and you can get a feel for what it might be like to share."

If I was willing to do poly, I'd still be wearing Master's collar. Tessa touched her bare neck again.

Marie leaned close enough to whisper. "I know. Not having a collar makes us feel naked, doesn't it. What time do you get off?"

"Not until seven. I have to close up."

"Okay. I'll go home and get dinner ready. I'll come back for you at seven and you can spend an evening with us. I'll drive you home whenever you want."

Tessa knew she should go home and make dinner for the man whose house she lived in. But, he wasn't her Master and if she called and let him know she had plans for the evening he wouldn't mind. "I guess."

Marie's grin lit up her face and Tessa couldn't help smiling back.

𝒰

After Tessa locked the shop's front door and turned toward the street, she fell back against the glass. Marie waited for her in the driver's seat of a mud splattered red Land Rover, the exact same model and color that Master drove. She stood frozen, the glass cold against her bare shoulders.

Marie stepped out and opened the passenger door.

Tessa shook her head, but Marie grabbed her hand and pulled her toward the SUV.

It could be a coincidence. It's the kind of car a Master would drive, especially if he liked taking his girl to remote areas and tying her to a tree. The memories made Tessa moist and she let Marie push her up into the passenger seat.

Marie chattered while she drove, but Tessa was too lost in her own thoughts to hear what she said or notice where they were going. Not until the Rover pulled into a garage did she look up and recognize the shelves full of camping and ski equipment. A tear crept down her cheek while Marie climbed out and came around to open Tessa's door. When Tessa didn't move, Marie turned her in the seat and Tessa slid down into Marie's arms.

"He really misses you and very much wants his pet back." Marie guided Tessa to the vestibule off the garage and helped her removed her jeans and tank top, hanging them on the hooks on the wall. Tessa kicked off her sandals and turned to find Marie had stripped off her top and was unzipping her leather pants. She had a black thorny rose tattooed on her breast and a jaguar striding across her kidneys on her back.

She followed the other woman into Master's study and they both knelt on the plush carpet at his feet, waiting for him to put down his book.

When Master peered at her over his reading glasses, Tessa's bent over so her face rested on the carpet her arms above her head.

"Good girl." Tessa didn't know which of them he meant.

Master reached forward and grabbed a fistful of Tessa's hair, pulling her into a kneeling position. He pulled some of Marie's ebony locks across Tessa's golden hair. "Nice. I like the contrast."

He turned to Tessa. "It's good to have you back where you belong, pet. Have you decided having a sister slave might be better than being alone?"

Tessa shrugged her shoulders.

Master crooked a finger at Marie and she crawled forward. Tessa cringed. Marie unzipped Master's fly and extracted his already semi-erect cock from his boxers. This was the part Tessa knew would be the hardest to bear -- watching anyone else please her Master.

Marie kissed his glans and licked the length of his rod from pubes to tip until it stood straight up. Weighing his heavy sack in one hand, she grasped the base of his cock in the other and plunged her lips down his shaft to her fingers. Master gasped and Tessa had to bite her lip to keep from bursting into tears.

Master stroked Marie's long, black hair. He crooked a finger of his other hand at Tessa and she crawled over to him, grateful he was even aware of her presence. While Marie's head bobbed up and down, Master grabbed a hunk of Tessa's hair and pulled her up so he could suck on her tit. He released Marie and grabbed Tessa's other nipple, twisting it until she gasped. So slowly that she didn't notice at first, his teeth sunk into the one in his mouth. Her breathing grew heavy and she could smell her own musk as well as Marie's. Hers had much more of a rich vanilla aroma than Tessa's own that Master had always described as honey sweet.

When Master came, Marie swallowed every drop. Tessa tried not to pout, but her lower lip crept out from her upper.

"Good, girl." Master patted Marie on the head. "Now, I want to see you two together."

"But, Sir?" Tessa sank back onto her heels.

"It's okay, pet." He reached out his hand and she rested her cheek against his palm. "You don't have to go muff diving since you're straight. You can close your eyes and pretend it's whoever you want between your legs."

"You, of course, Sir."

He chuckled and looked at Marie who had a big grin on her face.

"Thank you, Sir." She opened her arms and Tessa sighed and crawled into them. Marie's touch was delicate and Tessa was surprised to discover she liked the feel of another pair of tits pressed up against her own. Marie ran her hand up and down Tessa's back and stroked the sensitive flesh of her ass until she gasped. Tilting Tessa's chin up, Marie touched her lips to Tessa's. At first, she kept them tightly together, but Marie teased with her tongue until Tessa relented and parted them.

Marie tasted of coffee and peppermint. She ran her tongue along the inside of Tessa's lips while fondling one breast until she was gasping for breath. Easing her back onto the carpet, Marie kissed her way down Tessa's neck to her breasts, tickling them all over with the tip of her tongue and suckling on her nipples. Tessa suppressed the urge to wriggle her hips. Master didn't allow that.

Finally, Marie made her way along Tessa's belly to her cunt. Marie pulled her lips apart and dragged the full length of her tongue through Tessa's slit. She almost screamed. The woman had a piercing near the back of her tongue. When the ball hit Tessa's clit, she had to dig her fingers into the carpet to keep from coming. "Please, Sir," she gasped.

"You have permission to come as much as you want when you're with this one, pet."

Tessa let go and her body shook under Marie's expert ministrations. She convulsed on the carpet as Marie tormented her clit and thrust her tongue deep into Tessa's cunt. Vaguely aware of Master's scent, Tessa opened her mouth and he pushed his cock between her lips. Unable to give him the attention he deserved, she just kept her mouth shaped like an O so he could face fuck her while Marie kept stimulating the orgasm that wouldn't end. Tessa was still trembling when he shot his load deep into her throat and she had to concentrate on swallowing so she wouldn't choke.

"Nice." Master lifted her up into his arms and held her against his chest.

Marie wrapped her arms around Tessa and Master, pressing her breasts against Tessa's back. Tessa clung to Master, grateful she still had a place in his heart. Apparently, he had room enough for both of them. Rather than live without him, she would find room in hers.

Winners & Losers
What Happens in Vegas

By I.G. Frederick

Jeffery eyed the pile of chips he'd amassed over the past six hours. He hadn't won that much money the entire time he'd been in Vegas. Normally no more than a ten-dollar-a-hand-bettor, he'd thrown down fifty-dollar and then hundred-dollar chips on a single hand of blackjack and tipped the cocktail waitress more for a soft drink than he normally would add to a dinner bill.

With a thousand dollars on the table, Jeffery was horrified to see a pair of aces materialize in the small square on the green felt in front of him. He sighed with relief when the dealer turned up a three for himself. *No choice but to double down.* Even if he lost this hand, he would still be ahead by almost eight grand for the night.

Holding his breath, he watched a nine and then an eight land next to his aces. *Could be worse.* The dealer flipped over his hole card to reveal a jack. Jeffery gripped the cold hard glass of cola, the condensation dampening his fingers. The dealer paused, teasing his players, then pulled a queen from the deck.

Jeffery let out his breath in one, long sigh. He stood up and pocketed all but one of his chips which he pushed toward the dealer. *Getting too reckless. Better quit while I'm ahead.* He grabbed his backpack and strode over to the cashier's cage.

After sliding his winnings into his billfold, Jeffery slipped it into the front pocket of his slacks and kept his hand over it. Not until he stepped away from the cage did the cacophony of slot machines and gamblers shouting in celebration register. Smoke hung visibly thick over the flashing lights. As he headed toward the front desk, the scent of potatoes frying reminded him he hadn't eaten since gobbling a nutrition bar for breakfast and it was now almost ten at night. He passed by the fast food outlets and strode into the swankiest restaurant in the casino that was still open.

He perused the menu with one eye on the red-headed waitress who had a bosom that begged for a man to bury his face in it and hips one could grab onto if one were ramming into her which he had an overwhelming desire to do.

"What can I get you, hun?"

"Your juiciest steak, rare, and your biggest baked potato loaded with everything. If you'll share it with me, bring me a bottle of champagne."

She chuckled. "Hun, I can't drink while I'm working."

He set the menu at the chipped edge of the polished wooden table. "Then why don't you clock out, Lisa, and bring me two steaks, one for yourself." Her name badge was so close to those luscious tits, he couldn't miss it.

"I clock out, the boss fires me. I need the job more than I need a steak."

"What time do you get off?"

She looked him over from the worn cuffs on his leather jacket to the ragged, dark brown hair that hadn't known a scissors for more than month. "If you want to buy a woman to help you celebrate your winnings, I can give you a card for a reputable whorehouse that's only an hour from town."

"Not, looking for a hooker and I don't have a car."

"They'll pick you up. Let me get that steak started for you." She turned and headed back toward the kitchen. Jeffery watched the sashay of her hips, encased in black taffeta, until they disappeared behind the swinging doors from which emanated the odors of grease, garlic, and onions.

She returned with a basket of rolls in one hand, a plate of lettuce with one cucumber slice and one tomato wedge in the other, and a triple, steel, condiment holder dangling from the index finger of each hand. One by one, she set each item in front of him. "Thousand, Caesar, and ranch dressings," she said when she put the first condiment holder down. "Sour cream, chives, and bacon." She placed the second condiment holder off to the side. "Did you decide what you wanted to drink?"

"If I waited would you let me buy you a drink when you got off work?" He spooned ranch on his lettuce and pulled out the darker of the two rolls from the bread basket. "This isn't about getting laid, although you're one gorgeous woman. Just looking for the company of a woman who isn't trying to sell me something."

"Look, Mister..."

He extended his hand. She ignored it. "Jeffrey, please, call me Jeffrey."

"I spend thirty hours a week on my feet in this dump, half the time getting no tips because if you join the players' club you get comped to a prime rib dinner special. At the end of the night, I just want to go home and wash the grease and smoke out of my hair."

"What do you like to do when you're not slinging hash here?" Jeffrey slathered butter on his roll.

"Leave town." She grabbed a coffee pot from behind a partition and headed to one of the other tables. "Let me know when you decide what you want to drink."

Jeffery chewed through his ranch covered lettuce and both rolls without tasting them wondering why he was so determined to get Lisa's attention. Ten thousand dollars was enough money to finally go home to Chicago. It would tide him over until he found a job. The last thing he needed was an entanglement that would keep in him Sin City. But, something about the woman made him want to either stay or take her with him.

The sizzle and smell of steak on a metal plate interrupted his reverie and woke up his senses. Lisa even brought him another bread basket. The sirloin wasn't the best steak he had ever eaten, but it filled the hole in his gut dug by six hours of clenching as the cards turned over. He sliced into the potato and filed it with butter and sour cream before heaping spoonfuls of chives and bacon on it. If he wasn't ravenous, it would have made a meal in itself. He used the last roll to wipe up the juice from the steak and bits of buttery sour cream that had dripped out of his spud.

"I take it you haven't eaten for a while?" Lisa gathered up the cleaned plate, empty bread basket, salad dressings, and condiment cups bare except for streaks of sour cream and a few bits of chive. "Dessert?"

"Whatcha got?"

"Cheesecake, blueberry or coconut cream pie, ice cream, and I think there's some bread pudding left."

None sounded appealing, but at least if he ordered dessert, he could sit and watch Lisa's hips wriggle back and forth across the dining room. "Sure, I'll take a piece of cheesecake."

"Strawberry, blueberry, or pineapple topping?"

"Pineapple?" It was a question, but Lisa took it as an order and disappeared back through the swinging doors of the kitchen.

The cheesecake came out of a box and the pineapple out of a can. But pretending to savor it gave Jeffrey the chance, now that his hunger was assuaged, to observe Lisa navigate her half a dozen tables. She, kept coffee cups and water glasses full, empty plates cleared, and drinks replaced. Her hands were never empty, her feet never stopped moving, and every dish she brought from the kitchen was steaming hot.

He was disgusted every time he saw a couple slide out of a curved booth after a full dinner, drinks, and dessert and only toss a five-dollar chip on the table. Several times he saw the comp coupons left with no tip at all.

As table after table turned, Lisa's rosy complexion turned paler and her steps slowed. He saw pain etch lines around her eyes and she made more trips carrying fewer plates. Sometimes another waitress helped her bring out dishes to a table full of rowdy gamblers, but more often than not that woman had her own customers to wait on.

Just before midnight, Lisa stopped by his table. "I don't mind if you hang out here, but it would be helpful if I could close out your tab before I head home. And, no I don't want company."

The bill was just over twenty dollars. Jeffrey put a fifty on top of the check. "Keep the change."

"I told you I'm not ..."

"That's just your tip. For excellent service and to make up for some of the schlubs who stiffed you."

"Thanks." She reached for the money.

He put two fingers on the check before she could take that as well. "I don't suppose you would be interested in knowing that I give a pretty mean foot massage."

She shook her head.

"I can get a room upstairs, you can take a shower, and let me pamper you."

Leaning over to take away his remaining silverware, she whispered, "I'm going home. Alone. But, if you want a place to stay tonight, you're much better off across the street than here. They actually have a pool and the rooms are clean." She looked over her shoulder. "You didn't hear that from me."

"Look, Lisa, I know we don't know each other yet. But,

I won enough tonight to get out of this hell hole. Why don't you come with me?"

She snatched the bill out from under his fingers, her face looking like someone had fed her rotten meat.

"No strings."

Her ready-to-flee tension eased and she stared at him.

"I'll pay for your ticket and you can stay with me until you find a job and place of your own."

She tilted her head.

"I mean, I don't have a place yet. But, I have enough to get an apartment ..."

"I gotta take care of this," she waved the bill, "and clock out. Meet me outside the Casino Center entrance in ten minutes."

Jeffrey grinned and shouldered his backpack. He stopped at the men's room and after washing his hands splashed cold water on his face. Dark circles under his red-rimmed eyes made Lisa's reluctance to consider going out with him after work understandable. But, a ticket out of this miserable dump ... hell, in the last two months he probably would have fucked any old hag who offered him a ticket home. He stood up and looked at his reflection sideways. *Not that bad.* At least eating junk food, when he could afford it, and dinner at the Mission when he couldn't, hadn't gone to his belly. *Of course, when your only transportation is your own two feet and you rarely eat more than one meal a day, it's hard to put on much weight.*

When he walked out onto the street, the cool breeze of the dessert night pulled the sweat from his shirt. Lisa marched past him, heading south. "C'mon. Don't want to miss the last bus or we'll have to walk five miles. He followed her the seven blocks to the transit center trying to remember if he had anything smaller than a fifty in his pocket.

"We'd better stop so I can get change."

"No time. I'll spot you."

"We could take a cab."

"Just 'cause you were lucky tonight's no reason to get all

extravagant." She picked up her pace and they boarded the 108 just before it pulled out.

Twenty minutes later, he followed her off the bus and across Paradise Road. She walked several blocks east on Harmon, turning into a run down complex of three-story stucco buildings with tile roofs. The sign out front advertised weekly and monthly rates. He remembered living in a similar dump shortly after he sold back his return trip ticket, determined to make his fortune in Sin City. Then, even that became too expensive.

She walked up the metal railed cement stairs and along an open air passage to a door in dire need of paint. Inside resembled a hotel room more than an apartment. Worn industrial carpet had scattered cigarette burns, tattered floral curtains fell two inches short of the window bottom, and the furniture looked like it had been left behind from the fifties. One door opened into a bedroom just big enough for a queen-sized bed and the other into a bathroom with a tiled shower stall so small he wondered if Lisa's ample bosom and zaftig hips prevented her from turning around. A tiny table and two chairs sat against the wall opposite the "kitchen" -- a row of cabinets with a half-size fridge under the counter, a miniature range, and a tiny stainless sink.

Lisa pointed to the floral print sofa with wooden accents. "You can sleep there until we get out of here." She turned on an old Acer sitting on the cheap wood coffee table. "The complex has wifi. You can buy tickets while I take a shower. Unless you won more six figures, find a cheap fare even if we have to wait couple of weeks." She strode into the bathroom. "Rent's paid 'til the end of month."

The running water made Jeffery long for a shower himself. He sniffed his pits and grimaced. He found the browser on the tiny notebook. *Of course compared to what people are carrying around the casinos these days, this is huge.* He could afford one of those tablets, now. Or even a smart phone. But, Lisa was right. He needed to be frugal. Ten grand wouldn't last long and who knows how much time it would take him to get a job back in Chicago.

He had just found a last minute special that would get them both to O'Hare for less than $500 when Lisa emerged from the bathroom wrapped in a towel that barely covered her breasts and stopped just below the cleft between her thighs that he wanted desperately to taste.

Hovering over the buy button, reality smacked him in the face and he let out all his breath in a rush. "Found a good deal. Can't buy it though. No plastic." He kept his eyes on the screen, unable to meet her gaze. "Don't suppose you have a credit card? I know this sounds like I'm playing you." He pulled out his wallet. "But, I'll give you the cash right now."

"I only have a debit card and I don't have more than thirty bucks in my account. We'll have to go to the bank tomorrow and put in enough money to cover tickets."

Jeffrey looked up and found no condemnation or anger. He grinned. "Limited time offer, we'll probably lose it. But, I'm sure we can find something comparable. Now, about that foot massage I promised. Do you mind if I take a shower, first?"

"Go ahead. But, I'll probably be asleep by the time you finish. I'll leave a blanket and pillow out for you."

"Thanks, Lisa. Much appreciated."

He rummaged in his backpack until he found a pair of clean briefs, his last. After they went to the bank in the morning, he should buy some quarters and find a Laundromat.

Lingering under the hot water with barely enough room to lean down to wash his feet, he laughed at his stupidity. For the price of Lisa's ticket he could have paid for a week in a hotel room with a shower big enough to turn around in and slept in a bed instead of on some old lumpy sofa that probably reeked of cigarette smoke.

The bedroom light was still on when he emerged from the bathroom wearing only his briefs, his wet hair plastered to the back of his neck. He knocked on the half open door. "Sure

I can't talk you into that foot massage? Or a back rub?"

"I guess."

He pushed the door ajar. Lisa sat up in bed, propped up with pillows, reading a library book. She wore a black slip that barely contained her creamy breasts. Tossing the sheet that covered her from the waist down to one side, she pointed to the battered chest of drawers jammed between the bed and the wall next to a sliding closet door. "Lotion."

Jeffrey edged around the footboard that was only fourteen inches from the wall and grabbed the plastic bottle. Sitting on the edge of the bed, he poured the rose scented lotion into one palm and rubbed them together. He picked up Lisa's foot and resisted the urge to kiss it. Starting with the heal, he rubbed the lotion into her skin and the kinks out of her muscles. By the time he switched to her other foot, she'd slid down in the bed and closed her eyes.

He gave in to temptation and pressed his lips to the top of that foot, her skin soft against his, before he rubbed lotion into the heel.

"You're not bad. Maybe I will take you up on that back rub."

"My pleasure." When he finished with her feet, Jeffrey waited until Lisa turned over onto her stomach and pulled the straps of her slip down to her waist. He reached for the lotion, but changed his mind, leaned forward, and licked her skin from her waist to her neck. Lisa moaned and her hips wiggled. Knowing she couldn't see his face, Jeffrey smirked. Starting at her waist, he rubbed her back, massaging her muscles with his thumbs, kneading out the kinks he found with the heels of his hands.

Gradually another aroma overwhelmed the scent of roses from the lotion. Jeffrey leaned forward and licked Lisa's neck. She practically purred. He nibbled on her ear. She turned onto her side exposing the amazing tits that had drawn him to her in the first place.

"May I?" His hand floated just above her skin and he could feel the heat radiating off her.

She shrugged. "What the fuck. Now that you've got me all hot and bothered, you may as well ..."

He lowered his hand and caressed the silky skin, closing his eyes to immerse himself in her softness. With his hand fondling one glorious boob, he nuzzled the other with his lips, licking his way across her big brown areola to her hardened nipple. He slid his other hand along her back to her luscious ass, stroking her cheeks through the satiny slip.

The smell of her musk grew stronger and he pushed the slip up to gain access to her bare skin. She whimpered and he took that as a cue to kiss his way from her breast down her belly, pulling the slip out of his way as he went. Turning onto her back, she lifted her hips so he could remove the slip, and parted her legs.

Dragging his tongue through her ginger bush, he pushed it between her lips lapping up the juices dripping from her cunt. She shoved her quim up into his face and he dove in, finding her clit with his tongue and pushing two fingers inside her to press up against her g-spot.

"Oh, gods, yes."

He pushed harder and enveloped her hard nub with his lips, sucking on it until her entire body shook and she cried out. Without pulling his face from her delicious snatch, he slid his briefs down his legs, releasing his engorged cock, and kicked them off.

After he made Lisa come two more times, he lifted his head and looked at her. "Don't have any condoms, but I'm clean and safe. Had a vasectomy four years ago. Never had an STD."

She took a deep breath and for a moment he wondered if he'd be looking for the nearest all night drugstore. But, Lisa opened her arms and Jeffrey kissed his way back up her belly, across her magnificent tits, to her lips. She wrapped her arms around his back and her legs around his thighs. Plunging into her sopping wet cunt, he moaned himself. He hadn't had sex with a woman since before he'd left the windy city. Her tight, soaking twat engulfed his throbbing prick and he had to bite his lip to avoid shooting off too soon.

He wanted to slam into her again and again, but knew that he wouldn't last if he did, so he eased in and out, grinding his pubes against her clit until she screamed and shuddered in his arms. Kissing her hard, he filled her with his spunk. When they both finally stopped trembling, he eased onto his side, still holding her in his arms, her head nestled against his shoulder.

"Maybe when we get to Chicago we can stick together?"

"We'll see." She took a deep breath and went limp in his arms.

He smiled. Nothing could beat sleeping every night with her amazing knockers pressed against his chest. He drifted off himself.

Winners & Losers Stays in Vegas

By I.G. Frederick

In six hours, Jeffery had won almost a thousand dollars and lost all but forty. He put half of it on one more hand of blackjack and was horrified to see a pair of aces materialize in the small square on the green felt in front of him. He sighed with relief when the dealer turned up a three for himself. *No choice but to double down.* He put his last twenty-dollar chip next to his cards.

Holding his breath, he watched a nine and then an eight land next to his aces. *Could be worse.* The dealer flipped over his hole card to reveal a jack. Jeffery gripped the cold hard glass of cola, the condensation dampening his fingers. The dealer paused, teasing his players, then pulled an eight from the deck.

Jeffery watched in disbelief as the dealer picked up his cards and used them to drag his last two chips away.

"Place your bets." The dealer ran a hand across the table.

Jeffrey's was the only empty square. He rose and shrugged his shoulders. "Broke." He picked up his backpack and slunk away from the table. His stomach rumbled. The cacophony of slot machines and gamblers shouting in celebration mocked him. Smoke hung visibly thick over the flashing lights. As he headed toward the exit, the scent of potatoes frying reminded him he hadn't eaten today. He spotted a man typing into a phone. "Excuse me, Sir. Do you have the time?"

The man didn't even look up. "Nine fifty."

Jeffrey sighed. He'd missed dinner at the Mission. Shoving his hands in his pocket, he felt the piece of paper he'd stuffed in there hours ago. He'd wandered into this casino to kill time until the Mission opened and found a five dollar chip in the men's room. Taking it as an omen, he'd signed up for the players' club card and gotten a coupon. He pulled it out and salivated. Lifting his chin off his chest, he strode past the fast food outlets and got in line for the swankiest restaurant in the casino that was still open.

The red-headed waitress who came to take his order had a bosom that begged for a man to bury his face in it and hips one could grab onto if one were ramming into her which he had an overwhelming desire to do.

"What can I get you, hun?"

He showed her the coupon good for the $9.95 prime rib dinner special.

She sighed. "Anything to drink?"

He hung his head. "Sorry, this is all I have. I don't even have any money for a tip."

She took a deep breath. "Soup or salad?"

He looked up. "Salad please, Lisa." Her name badge was so close to those luscious tits, he couldn't miss it.

She looked him over from the worn cuffs on his leather jacket to the ragged, dark brown hair that hadn't known a scissors for more than month and headed back toward the kitchen. Jeffery watched the sashay of her hips, encased in black taffeta, until they disappeared behind the swinging doors from which emanated the odors of grease, garlic, and onions. He emptied his water glass in two gulps.

Lisa returned with a basket of rolls in one hand, a plate of lettuce with one cucumber slice and one tomato wedge in the other, and a triple, steel, condiment holder dangling from the index finger of each hand. One by one, she set each item in front of him. "Thousand, Caesar, and ranch dressings," she said when she put the first condiment holder down. "Sour cream, chives, and bacon for your potato." She placed the second condiment holder off to the side. He spooned ranch on his lettuce and pulled out the darker of the two rolls from the bread basket. After slathering on butter, he gobbled it in two bites. By the time Lisa returned with the pitcher to fill his water glass, he had cleared his salad plate and finished both rolls.

Lisa didn't ask if he wanted more bread, she just brought him another basket. Knowing the best he could hope for was dinner at the Mission tomorrow evening, he devoured two of the three rolls in it without tasting them before the smell of meat woke up his senses. The prime rib wasn't the best he had ever eaten, but it filled the hole in his gut dug by six hours of clenching as the cards turned over. He sliced into the potato and filed it with butter and sour cream before heaping spoonfuls of chives and bacon on it. If he wasn't ravenous, it would have made a meal in itself. He used the last roll to wipe up the juice from the steak and bits of buttery sour cream that had dripped out of his spud.

"I take it you haven't eaten for a while?" Lisa gathered up the cleaned plate, empty bread basket, salad dressings, and condiment cups bare except for streaks of sour cream and a few bits of chive.

He nodded. "Wish I could afford dessert."

Leaning over to take away his remaining silverware, she whispered, "If you don't tell anyone, I'll throw in a piece of cheesecake. We've got too much left tonight and it'll just get tossed out at the end of the shift."

He grinned. Dessert would also give him more time to sit and watch Lisa's hips wriggle back and forth across the dining room. "Sure, thanks."

"Strawberry, blueberry, or pineapple topping?"

"Pineapple?" It was a question, but Lisa took it as an order and disappeared back through the swinging doors of the kitchen.

The cheesecake came out of a box and the pineapple out of a can. But he reached satiety for the first time in months. Pretending to savor his dessert gave Jeffrey the chance to observe Lisa navigate her half a dozen tables. She kept coffee cups and water glasses full, empty plates cleared, and drinks replaced. Her hands were never empty, her feet never stopped moving, and every dish she brought from the kitchen was steaming hot.

He was disgusted every time he saw a couple slide out of a curved booth after a full dinner, drinks, and dessert and only toss a five-dollar chip on the table. Several times he saw the comp coupons left with no tip at all and hung his head.

When he scraped the last of the graham cracker crumbs off his plate, Lisa stopped by to remove it. He set the coupon at the chipped edge of the polished wooden table. "Has anyone ever told you that you're one gorgeous woman?"

"Look, Mister ..."

He extended his hand. She ignored it. "Jeffrey, please, call me Jeffrey. I don't suppose you would be interested in knowing that I give a pretty mean foot massage."

She shook her head. "I spend thirty hours a week on my feet in this dump, half the time getting no tips because of those damned coupons. At the end of the night, I just want to go home and wash the grease and smoke out of my hair."

"What do you like to do when you're not slinging hash here?"

"Leave town." She grabbed a coffee pot from behind a partition and headed off.

As table after table turned, Lisa's rosy complexion turned

paler and her steps slowed. He saw pain etch lines around her eyes and she made more trips carrying fewer plates. Sometimes another waitress helped her bring out dishes to a table full of rowdy gamblers, but more often than not that woman had her own customers to wait on.

Just before midnight, Lisa stopped by his table. "I take it you're hanging out here because you have nowhere else to go?"

He reached for his pack. "I'll leave. I really wish I had the money to give you a tip. The service was beyond excellent. I just can't believe how many schlubs stiffed you."

"I'm used to it."

"That doesn't make it right. I really do give good foot massages. I don't suppose you'd let me give you one in lieu of a tip?"

Her face looking like someone had fed her rotten meat. "I'm going home. Alone. I really don't want company."

"I'm not trying to hit on to you, honest. It's just that's all I have to offer."

Her ready-to-flee tension eased and she stared at him.

"We can go sit on one of the benches on Fremont. No chance of me taking advantage of you."

"I'd miss my bus home."

He sighed.

She tilted her head.

"I gotta clock out. Meet me outside the Casino Center entrance in ten minutes."

Jeffrey grinned and shouldered his backpack. He stopped at the men's room and after washing his hands splashed cold water on his face. Dark circles under his red-rimmed eyes made Lisa's reluctance to consider letting him touch her understandable. He stood up and looked at his reflection sideways. *Not that bad.* At least eating junk food, when he could afford it, and dinner at the Mission when he couldn't, hadn't gone to his belly. *Of course, when your only transportation is your own two feet and you're lucky to eat one meal a day, it's hard to put on much weight.*

When he walked out onto the street, the cool breeze of the dessert night pulled the sweat from his shirt. Lisa marched past him, heading south. "C'mon. Don't want to miss the last bus or I'll have to walk five miles. He followed her the seven blocks to the transit center before he realized he couldn't even scratch up the two-dollar fare.

"I don't have bus fare."

"I'll spot you." She picked up her pace and they boarded the 108 just before it pulled out. Much to Jeffrey's chagrin, she extracted two singles from her pocket and slid them into the fare box, flashing a pass for herself.

Twenty minutes later, he followed her off the bus and across Paradise Road. She walked several blocks east on Harmon, turning into a run down complex of three-story stucco buildings with tile roofs. The sign out front advertised weekly and monthly rates. He remembered living in a similar dump shortly after he sold back his return trip ticket, determined to make his fortune in Sin City. Then, even that became too expensive.

She walked up the metal railed cement stairs and along an open air passage to a door in dire need of paint. Inside resembled a hotel room more than an apartment. Worn industrial carpet had scattered cigarette burns, tattered floral curtains fell two inches short of the window bottom, and the furniture looked like it had been left behind from the fifties. One door opened into a bedroom just big enough for a queen-sized bed and the other into a bathroom with a tiled shower stall so small he wondered if Lisa's ample bosom and zaftig hips prevented her from turning around. A tiny table and two chairs sat against the wall opposite the "kitchen" -- a row of cabinets with a half-size fridge under the counter, a miniature range, and a tiny stainless sink.

Lisa pointed to the floral print sofa with wooden accents. "You can sleep there tonight." She turned on an old Acer sitting on the cheap wood coffee table. "The complex has wifi. You can check out employment options while I take a shower." She strode into the bathroom.

The running water made Jeffery long for a shower himself. He sniffed his pits and grimaced. He found the browser on the tiny notebook. *Of course compared to what people are carrying around the casinos these days, this is huge.* Every job listing he saw wanted experience he didn't have and expected a resume with a mailing address, a phone number, and an e-mail.

Lisa emerged from the bathroom wrapped in a towel that barely covered her breasts and stopped just below the cleft between her thighs that he wanted desperately to taste.

"Nobody on craigslist looking for lousy card players with only eight years as an Army grunt for experience." He closed the browser. "Can't even apply for manual labor without an address or a phone and I don't have either."

Jeffrey looked up and found no condemnation or anger.

"Have you tried the employment office? I think they offer a message service and there's gotta be training options for veterans."

"To be honest, I never even thought about looking for a job here." He turned off the computer. "I came here for a week to celebrate escaping two tours without getting shipped to the Middle East. Got lucky. Thought I could win enough playing blackjack to make a living. Then I was just hoping for enough to get back home on."

"You're not alone."

He looked up at her, wet strands of her hair clung to her creamy white shoulders.

She shook her head. "Born and raised here. Couldn't afford college and grades weren't good enough to get a scholarship so slinging hash, as you call it, is pretty much my only option." She sighed. "When I was younger and could get gigs wearing those teensy outfits and delivering drinks to the high rollers in the Strip casinos, I made a decent living. But as I got older, \I gained weight and my feet gave out. I couldn't wear the required high heels anymore, so I'm stuck working at dumps downtown."

"About that foot massage I promised. Do you mind if I take a shower, first?"

"Go ahead. But, I'll probably be asleep by the time you finish. I'll leave a blanket and pillow out for you."

"Thanks, Lisa. Much appreciated. I get so very tired of the preaching over at the Mission, when they even have an open bed." He rummaged in his backpack until he found a pair of clean briefs, his last.

Even with barely enough room to lean down to wash his feet, lingering under the hot water was a luxurious treat. Hell, sleeping on some old lumpy sofa that probably reeked of cigarette smoke beat a hard wooden bench and getting rousted by the cops or a cot at the Mission listening to dozens of other men snore and wheeze.

The bedroom light was still on when he emerged from the bathroom wearing only his briefs, his wet hair plastered to the back of his neck. He knocked on the half open door. "Sure I can't talk you into that foot massage? Or a back rub?"

"I guess."

He pushed the door ajar. Lisa sat up in bed, propped up with pillows, reading a library book. She wore a black slip that barely contained her creamy breasts. Tossing the sheet that covered her from the waist down to one side, she pointed to the battered chest of drawers jammed between the bed and the wall next to a sliding closet door. "Lotion."

Jeffrey edged around the footboard that was only fourteen inches from the wall and grabbed the plastic bottle. Sitting on the edge of the bed, he poured the rose scented lotion into one palm and rubbed them together. He picked up Lisa's foot and resisted the urge to kiss it. Starting with the heal, he rubbed the lotion into her skin and the kinks out of her muscles. By the time he switched to her other foot, she'd slid down in the bed and closed her eyes.

He gave in to temptation and pressed his lips to the top of that foot, her skin soft against his, before he rubbed lotion into the heel.

"You're not bad. Maybe I will take you up on that back rub."

"My pleasure." When he finished with her feet, Jeffrey waited until Lisa turned over onto her stomach and pulled the straps of her slip down to her waist. He reached for the lotion, but changed his mind, leaned forward, and licked her skin from her waist to her neck. Lisa moaned and her hips wiggled. Knowing she couldn't see his face, Jeffrey smiled. Starting at her waist, he rubbed her back, massaging her muscles with his thumbs, kneading out the kinks he found with the heels of his hands.

Gradually another aroma overwhelmed the scent of roses from the lotion. Jeffrey leaned forward and licked Lisa's neck. She practically purred. He nibbled on her ear. She turned onto her side exposing the amazing tits that had drawn him to her in the first place.

"May I?" His hand floated just above her skin and he could feel the heat radiating off her.

She shrugged. "What the fuck. Now that you've got me all hot and bothered, you may as well ..."

He lowered his hand and caressed the silky skin, closing his eyes to immerse himself in her softness. With his hand fondling one glorious boob, he nuzzled the other with his lips, licking his way across her big brown areola to her hardened nipple. He slid his other hand along her back to her luscious ass, stroking her cheeks through the satiny slip.

The smell of her musk grew stronger and he pushed the slip up to gain access to her bare skin. She whimpered and he took that as a cue to kiss his way from her breast down her belly, pulling the slip out of his way as he went. Turning onto her back, she lifted her hips so he could remove the slip, and parted her legs.

Dragging his tongue through her ginger bush, he pushed it between her lips lapping up the juices dripping from her cunt. She shoved her quim up into his face and he dove in, finding her clit with his tongue and pushing two fingers inside her to press up against her g-spot.

"Oh, gods, yes."

He pushed harder and enveloped her hard nub with his lips, sucking on it until her entire body shook and she cried out. Without pulling his face from her delicious snatch, he slid his briefs down his legs, releasing his engorged cock, and kicked them off.

After he made Lisa come two more times, he lifted his head and looked at her. "Don't have any condoms, but I'm clean and safe. Got a vasectomy between tours. Never had an STD."

She took a deep breath and for a moment he wondered if she'd be sending him to the nearest all night drugstore. But, Lisa opened her arms and Jeffrey kissed his way back up her belly, across her magnificent tits, to her lips. She wrapped her arms around his back and her legs around his thighs. Plunging into her sopping wet cunt, he moaned himself. He hadn't had sex with a woman since before he'd left the windy city. Her tight, soaking twat engulfed his throbbing prick and he had to bite his lip to avoid shooting off too soon.

He wanted to slam into her again and again, but knew that he wouldn't last if he did, so he eased in and out, grinding his pubes against her clit until she screamed and shuddered in his arms. Kissing her hard, he filled her with his spunk. When they both finally stopped trembling, he eased onto his side, still holding her in his arms, her head nestled against his shoulder.

"If you'd consider letting me stay with you until I get back on my feet, I'll make sure you never have to sling hash again. I promise, no more cards."

"We'll see." She took a deep breath and went limp in his arms.

He smiled. Anything would be worth it to sleep every night with her amazing knockers pressed against his chest. He drifted off himself.

Acknowledgements

This book would not have reached your hands without the help of many dear friends and colleagues. I thank my readers and supporters, especially Cindy, my proofreader, editor, and best friend. Thanks also to all those who have served me, well and ill, over the years. I have learned something from each one of you and I hope that you find what you seek.

Other fiction
by I.G. Frederick includes:

Complicated Couplings

Four sexy stories about tangled twosomes

"If You Love Someone" — Tara leaves her husband to move in with Nathan, but he abandons her after a few months. When he returns, begging her to take him back, life and love look very different.

"Commiserate" — The same man dumped them both. When they commiserate, they discover more in common than an ex-boyfriend.

"Passion's Price" — Richard steals Gina's heart from three thousand miles away. But, when he moves across the country, her intensity and passion for life drive him away.

"Lunchtime Lover" — Both married, they started their affair with the promise never to fall in love. Then Lisa's divorce becomes final.

www.eroticawriter.net/ComplicatedCouplings.html

Cougar Conquests

Beautiful older women on the prowl and the sweet young cubs captured by their allure

"Benjamin" — A chance meeting at a munch in a tiny town leads Benjamin to an opportunity for training. But, Lady Gina tries to end the relationship rather than emotionally torture herself.

"Festival of Eros" — The handsome young man followed her around all evening, behaving like the perfect submissive ... until she learned his identity.

"Paddles" — A biker bar with no bikers? The decor, name, and patrons of a bar in a small Eastern Oregon town puzzle William who just stopped in for a beer. Then the owner introduces him to the secrets of this very special tavern.

"Starting Over" - When her pet walked out on her, she stayed away from parties because it hurt to watch other women playing with their toys. But, a friend coerces her into attending a unique event.

"The Cougar and the College Boys" — Alone in the woods, hours from Portland, Tess discovers four college friends staying in a nearby cabin. The boys invite her to share their campfire, their dinner, and ...

www.eroticawriter.net/CougarConquests.html

WARNING:

This book changes women's attitudes about relationship dynamics, forever.

In Geneviéve's journey of discovery she dabbles in the BDSM lifestyle which forces her to recognize and acknowledge her true nature. Her memoir, woven together with that of a male slave, draws the reader into an intense odyssey of sexual expression triumphing over sexual repression while delivering fascinating insight about a different kind of love.

"The aptly titled Dommemoir *delivers on so many levels... It quickly sucks you in and envelopes you in the bondage of its spell...* Dommemoir *is a character study that breathes complex and compelling life into its hero, the devastating Lady Geneviéve and the fortunate submissives who worship at her feet... placing you in the delicious bondage of its dark and compelling landscape..."*

Larry Brooks, USA Today bestselling author of Darkness Bound **and** Bait and Switch

www.eroticawriter.net/Dommemoir.html

Eleanor & Mick

A journey of sexual exploration and insight

In five sizzling hot stories, Eleanor seeks refuge in a small town on the Oregon Coast and befriends her younger neighbor. He captures first her heart and then her submission, taking her on a journey of sexual exploration and insight.

"Salt for His Wounds" — When Eleanor's ex-husband shows up begging for a second chance, she asks her young, gorgeous next door neighbor for a favor and Mick takes advantage of the opportunity.

"The Mercantile" — Eleanor attributes Mick's detachment to the difference in their ages, but Mick confesses a need for kink. Afraid of losing him, Eleanor reluctantly consents to bondage and pain.

"The Things We Do for Love" — When her gorgeous girlfriend visits Eleanor on the coast, Mick's obvious attraction troubles her. But, Liz only has eyes for Eleanor.

"Paid in Full" — Mick's army buddy finds Eleanor hot and makes a deal with Mick. But, if Mick really loved Eleanor would he let another man have sex with her?

"Renovations" — After Mick spends a month renovating their garage, Eleanor discovers he built in a few surprises.

www.eroticawriter.net/EleanorMick.html

Family Dynamics

Six sultry stories exploring sexuality in Dominant/submissive liaisons

"'Aunt' Grace" — Jen needed a place to stay in Portland and turned to her father's stepsister. But, she found so much more than she ever dreamed possible with her "Aunt" Grace. *Second Place, NLA:I John Preston Short Story Award.*

"Leather Family" — Kyle needs his own boy. Jacques would do almost anything to find a place in a Leather Family. But, Kyle serves a female Master.

"Searching" — Two dominants love each other, but need someone who submits to them both. Just how far will young Jeremy go to serve the lovely Lady Theresa?

"Taking Control" — To free the woman she loves from a horrid sadist's perverted games, Melanie must set aside her own aversion to men.

"Family Ties" — When her slave's ex faces eviction, Katherine offers refuge. But can Naomi pay the price?

"Said the Unicorn" — Tessa dedicates herself to her Master's service, so his determination to add another woman to their family devastates her.

www.eroticawriter.net/FamilyDynamics.html

Ladies in Love

Six sizzling stories of Lesbian Lust

"Empty Seat" — *Laura offers Alex a nightcap as thanks for help with a presentation to a prospective client. But they never order drinks.*

"'Aunt' Grace" — *Jen needed a place to stay in Portland and turned to her father's stepsister. But, she found so much more than she ever dreamed possible with her "Aunt" Grace. Second Place, NLA:I John Preston Short Story Award.*

"Spa Date" — *Dismayed that she introduced Sam to the woman who betrayed her, Julie tries to fix her up again.*

"Taking Control" — *To free the woman she loves from a horrid sadist's perverted games, Melanie must set aside her own aversion to men.*

"Dental School" — *How can Cindy flirt with the beautiful blonde dental instructor while her mother propositions the student examining her teeth on Cindy's behalf?*

"Commiserate" — *The same man dumped them both. When they commiserate, they discover more in common than an ex-boyfriend.*

www.eroticawriter.net/LadiesinLove.html

Lessons Learned
Sometimes you need more than love

Four sizzling hot FemDom love stories about women who come to terms with their dominant sides and discover that makes them more attractive to the men they love.

"Tea Party" — What if the first time your best friend drags you to a FemDom "Tea Party" you see your former boyfriend serving canapes naked?

"Blind Date" — How do you respond when you find your ex-husband hanging out at the restaurant where you planned to meet your "Blind Date"?

"To Serve" — If you love a vanilla woman and you only want "To Serve," how do you introduce her to the lifestyle without scaring her away?

"Change in View" — What if a "Change in View" alters the attitude of the man you mentored so he could find his perfect Mistress?

www.eroticawriter.net/LessonsLearned.html

Love Hurts
but in a good way
five steamy stories about the dark side of love

"B&D Trainee" —Online, Xavier promised to make his B&D fantasies come true. But, had he jumped in over his head?

"Knife Play" — Seeking a knife he saw online, Jack

inadvertently found himself in a room full of pain and bondage contraptions. He almost turned around and left, but a beautiful woman taught him a different way to appreciate blades.

"Pussy Whipped" — *Eric knew nothing about BDSM, but purchased a ticket to a fundraiser to help out his friends. When Miranda asks him to "play," he discovers exactly what those four letters mean.*

"The Auction" — *He attended the auction with only one goal — to acquire a very special whip. But an offer to try it out proved irresistible and he discovered sometimes events, and women, can exceed one's expectations.*

"FemDom Fairy Tale" — *A FemDom's offhand remark about a photograph at an erotic art show draws a handsome man's attention. But, when two dominants find each other attractive, which one chooses to kneel?*

www.eroticawriter.net/LoveHurts.html

Second Chances

Six sexy stories about getting a second shot at the gold ring

"Back to School" — *An admin error forces Jordan and Dennis to share a dorm room. Older than their classmates, they decide to stick together. But Jordan's past threatens to keep them apart.*

"Gordon" — *When the cover model of her latest book walks into the coffee shop where she writes, Lenore embarrassingly calls him by her character's name. His reaction confounds her.*

"Spa Date" — Dismayed that she introduced Sam to the woman who betrayed her, Julie tries to fix her up again.

"Salt for His Wounds" — When Eleanor's ex-husband shows up begging for a second chance, she asks her young, gorgeous next door neighbor for a favor. Mick takes advantage of the opportunity.

"Proposal — Tangled Webs" — The evening appears perfectly arranged for him to pop the question. But, Christopher's proposition takes Geraldine on an un-anticipated sexual adventure.

"Starting Over" — When her pet walked out on her, she stayed away from parties because it hurt to watch other women playing with their toys. But, a friend co-erces her into attending a unique event.

www.eroticawriter.net/SecondChances.html

When Two's Not Enough
Seven sexy ménage stories

"Tribal Fusion" — Whenever and wherever he dances, Dominic collects propositions, but the Lady Lenore's proposal takes him by surprise.

"Two Brothers" — A divorcée in a flashy sports car attracts the attention of two young virgin brothers visiting the "big" city of Boise.

"Honeymoon" — Although she expected to honey-moon aboard a cruise ship, Allison finds herself sail-ing on a private yacht staffed by an incredibly beauti-ful couple. Believing her new husband wants to hide his older, less attractive wife, makes it difficult to enjoy the hedonistic delights offered in paradise.

"Jail Bait" — Serena wants Joshua to pop her cherry, but he won't touch her because of her age. When her birthday finally makes it legal, he arranges for a very special celebration.

"Nikki's Birthday" — Even someone happy in a monogamous relationship might find the gift of a hot, new toy for an evening of decadence incredibly exciting.

"Market Boy" — When a beautiful Domme offers Jack the opportunity to serve at a party for her friends, he responds too quickly and too eagerly, getting more than he bargained for.

"The Cougar and the College Boys" — Alone in the woods, hours from Portland, Tess discovers four college friends staying in a nearby cabin. The boys invite her to share their campfire, their dinner, and ...

www.eroticawriter.net/TwoNotEnough.html

Young & Eager
Barely legal but hardly innocent

"Two Brothers" — A divorcée in a flashy sports car attracts the attention of two young virgin brothers visiting the "big" city of Boise.

"Teachers Pet" — Trapped at an all-girls' school in the middle of nowhere, Sabrina tries to get her hunky teacher to bust her cherry.

"Arresting Development" — *Bethany went out with Officer Rick to avoid a speeding ticket, but discovered she enjoyed getting "arrested."*

"Jail Bait" — *Serena wants Joshua to pop her cherry, but he won't touch her because of her age. When her birthday finally makes it legal, he arranges for a very special celebration.*

www.eroticawriter.net/YoungEager.html

Or visit
http://eroticawriter.net/
to find links to individual stories
and additional collections
and

For darker, edgier fiction look for books by

KORIN DUSHAYL

The Darker Side of Intimacy

transgressivewriter.com